# Lighten Up

# Lighten Up

by

Ashley Davis

This is a work of fiction. Names, characters,
businesses, places, events, locales, and
incidents are either the products of the
author's imagination or used in a fictitious
manner. Any resemblance to actual persons,
living or dead, or actual events is purely
coincidental.

Printed in the United States of America

First Printing, 2020

ISBN: 978-1-951883-28-7

Butterfly Typeface Publishing
PO Box 56193
Little Rock, AR 72215

"I wondered if they were just smiling
faces hating other races."

To the families and friends mourning the loss of your loved ones:

I'm grieving with you.

I'm keeping you in my prayers.

May God comfort you

and help you find peace as the days go by.

# Table of Contents

## Introduction

"Mama, I don't want to be Black anymore. Black is not beautiful like you said. Black is bad. Black is ugly. Black is why daddy's gone."

"Come here, sweetheart. I miss daddy too, but Black is not the problem. Everything I told you is still true. We are beautiful, and we are not bad. This world is bad. Just remember that. Daddy would not want you to feel this way."

Those words still haunt me to this day. That was 12 years ago. Although I was only four at the time, I made myself a promise that day, and I have kept it ever since.

---

*Chapter One*

---

"Renee, hurry up in the bathroom. You're gonna be late for school!"

"Ok, Mom, I'll be out in a minute."

Ten more minutes passed before I finally made it to the dining room table. My mom had turned around right before I walked into the room. I hung my head as I ate because I knew she would yell at me if she saw me.

"Good morning, Renee. Did you forget your manners in the bathroom?"

"I'm sorry, Mom. Good morning."

"Let me see your beautiful face."

"I can't. I'll be late for school."

Still, my mom wouldn't take no for an answer. She looked at me and saw that I had packed on makeup ten shades lighter than I was.

"Go wash your face off immediately, Renee. This is unnecessary. You do not need to hide your complexion. Why cover it up?"

"You wouldn't understand," and I was right. She wouldn't. She couldn't.

My dad's death affected us very differently. My mom saw it as a reason to embrace her blackness, but I didn't want to embrace anything but a different color, any other color. I knew my dad would still be alive if he looked like someone else. His only "crime" was driving while Black, and that was enough to make him lose his life. My mom could never understand what seeing that did to me.

I watched as my dad was pulled over for no reason. I saw the look of panic in his eyes and the sweat beading down his neck. I watched as the officer, Roger Callahan, told my father to get his license and registration. I saw my dad keep one hand in the air while he reached for his wallet, and as soon as he did, I heard a noise that sounded like popping balloons. The next sound I heard was my mom's screams as she said, "Why, Lord, why! Jesus no! Jesus, I can't! He was just reaching for his wallet like you told him to. Why'd you have to shoot him?"

With a blank expression on his face, the officer didn't respond. He turned to walk away when he locked eyes with me.

He stood there for a while listening to me saying, "Daddy? Daddy, are you ok? Daddy, answer me."

"I love you, baby girl. Remember, daddy loves you."

My daddy died on the spot, and my life has been in shambles since.

"Hurry up, Renee! The bus is outside."

"Mom, when can I get a car? I hate riding on the bus."

"We'll talk about it when you get home." She said as she hugged me.

She always said that, and whenever I got home, she changed the subject. I knew she didn't want me driving because of people like Officer Callahan, racist cops who lived to target Black lives.

Although I understood where she was coming from, I just wanted to experience what freedom was like, but my mom didn't know how to let me do that.

I loved my mom very much, but my dad's death drove a wedge between us instead of bringing us closer together.

Thankfully, I had the support of my friends, and I didn't need to wait for my mom to understand.

I waved goodbye to my mom as I got on the bus.

"Find a seat, Renee. We are running late." The bus driver said.

"Yes ma'am," I said as I walked to the nearest open seat.

"Hi, can you please scoot over? This is the only empty seat on the bus." I asked.

"No, I don't want to sit by you. Go sit in your section." Aiden replied grinning from ear to ear.

"My section?" I asked. Then, I turned to see where he was pointing.

When I looked, he was pointing at the Black people all sitting together.

"No, move over now. I'm not sitting with them."

"With them? You are a them. Don't think I don't see you trying to lighten up. You're not fooling anyone." He rolled his eyes and begrudgingly moved over when he locked eyes with the bus driver.

"Thank you for moving," I said as I sat down and turned my body to face the aisle.

On the way to school, I reapplied my makeup. I had been experimenting with lighter shades hoping to find the one that best suited me.

When the bus pulled into the parking lot and stopped, everyone was staring at me.

"What? It's not polite to stare." I said as I got up and ran to the bus door.

"Miss White, the bus driver, grabbed me by the arm and said, "Honey, you are beautiful. You do not need to change your complexion. You are perfect just the way you are."

I was not in the mood for a debate, so I just nodded and walked off of the bus. My friends were waiting for me by the school steps.

"Hey, Renee."

"Hey, Emmitt. Hey, Nyssa."

"Guess what, Renee," Emmitt said with glee.

"What?"

"I finally got a car! Over the weekend, my parents told me I could pick any car I wanted under 25k. I debated getting a new car, but I got a certified used vehicle with maximum warranties instead."

"Well, what car did you get? Don't leave me hanging."

Emmitt pulled the keys out of his pocket and pushed the lock button. I heard the sound coming from the right side of the lot, and when I looked, I saw lights flashing on a Ford Mustang GT.

"No way! You got your dream car? Congratulations!"

"Thanks, Renee. Do you know what else that means?"

"No, what does it mean?"

"It means you don't have to ride the bus anymore!"

I was so excited. I gave Emmitt the biggest hug.

"Emmitt Grey, you are a life-saver!"

---

*Chapter Two*

---

"Everyone, come in and take a seat. Students, get settled. We have a guest speaker today. When the bell rings, we will meet in the gym. Make sure you listen carefully to everything the speaker says because you will be tested on the information." Mr. Brown said.

We all chatted while we waited for the bell to ring. Usually, we would have gotten in trouble, but Mr. Brown knew that he didn't have enough time to teach us anything, so he left us alone.

*Ring Ring*

"Everyone, please line up single file in front of the door." Mr. Brown stood up and walked next to the line with his clipboard to make sure no one had the opportunity to skip the assembly.

"I wonder what this is all about. The school has never had a surprise assembly." I said with concern.

"It's probably something serious. They wouldn't cancel all of our classes just for the sake of it." Nyssa replied.

As I looked down the hall at other students lining up, I noticed that some of them were crying, and an awful feeling filled the pit of my stomach.

"Guys, something is definitely wrong." I stated assuredly.

One by one each student line entered the gym doors. Once we were all inside and seated, our principal, Mr. Black addressed us all.

"All right everyone, stand to your feet."

As we all stood, Mr. Black started our school cheer.

"Andrew McGill!"

"Fighting Bills!

"Andrew McGill!"

Fighting Bills!

"Fighting Bills! Fighting Bills! Fight your fight like Andrew McGill!"

Once we were all seated, Mr. Black began,

"Hello student body of Andrew McGill High, it is good to see you all here. There will be no classes today. We will be having a special speaker. After the speaker, we will have bond-building activity time and support groups available for students and faculty. Today's speaker is Mrs. James. She is here to speak to all of you about a problem that society is facing. Please welcome Mrs. James."

"Hello students," she said with a sad expression on her face.

"My name is Mrs. James, and my son, Kyrie, was a student at this school."

*Wait,* I thought to myself. *Did he graduate? Is she pulling him out of the school?*

"My beautiful brown baby boy was killed last night on his way home. I'm not sure how many of you have seen the videos on Watchlook, but he was pulled over for a broken taillight. The footage shows my baby responding politely to the officer just like my husband and I had taught him to do. He put his license and registration on the dash before the officer made it to the car, and he kept both hands on the wheel. The officer was clearly disgruntled based on his tone. He made my baby get out of his car and said, 'I don't need those things. I need to know who you stole this car from.' My son responded, 'This is my father's car, sir. I can give you his number to call.' When Kyrie walked back to the vehicle, he grabbed his phone and turned to face the officer. The officer shot him five times unaware that my son had called us before the officer had a chance to approach him. We heard as Kyrie's body hit the ground. He lost his life needlessly. My boy was not a threat. The officer is still walking the streets right now pending investigation." She took a deep breath and tried to compose herself.

"I came here today to let you know that my boy was a good boy. He was the captain of the varsity basketball team here. He was an honor student with a 4.8 GPA. He was a part of the Buds program. He was a son and a friend. He was active in the community, and most of all, he was a lover of Christ. I know my baby is in Heaven, but I didn't want to have to see him make it there before I did. Students, make sure that you comply with the police. Make sure that you live good lives. Do not give anyone a reason to think less of you than you are. You are all beautiful no matter what your race, creed, or ethnicity is. You could have been born any color, but God made you the color you are for a reason. Do not take that for granted. Do not take that lightly, and do not take that to mean that you can do whatever you want to do. No one is above anyone else. We are one." Mrs. James paused momentarily and said, "Thank you all for listening."

As she walked off of the platform, we erupted with applause. Listening to her story and the sound of pain in her voice reminded me of my mom when she spoke to a crowd of people during the Protest for Justice held in my father's name. It reminded me of the three weeks when my father's name was a hashtag. Everywhere I looked I saw #JusticeforMartin #SpeakHisName #MartinWilson.

Although I was young, I still watched the news with my mother. I was present at the protest. The world, or so I thought, was enraged by my father's death. Justice was called for, but I still don't think justice was received. Roger Callahan lost his job. He was sentenced to eight years in prison. At 12-years-old, I saw his release from prison on the local news. I could not believe that he was free just like that.

My Uncle Jordan is still in prison to this day for stealing a TV from Walkin's World. However, he stole nothing. The cashier forgot to give him the receipt, and he happened to walk out at the same time as another shopper with a TV. When the alarm sounded, my uncle was immediately stopped, but the other shopper was able to leave the store without question or suspicion. Walkin's was known for firing employees who forgot to give receipts to customers, so the employee never came forward to stop him from being arrested. My uncle's name matched a known felon the same age as he was who had multiple counts of theft on his record. The prosecution argued that my uncle was the felon in the mugshots presented to the judge and jury.

Uncle Jordan received a ten-year sentence when I was 7-years-old. It made no sense to me. What happened to my father was an act of violence. My uncle didn't do anything wrong, but he received a harsher punishment. It hurt me tremendously to see him hauled off to prison. He was my uncle, but he was also like a father to me. Uncle Jordan was so much like my actual father. He had the same mannerisms, and they even spoke the same way. Losing him to the system broke what was left of my heart. It felt like the last piece of my father had been taken away, and now, I had nothing left of him. These were the reasons I refused to be Black anymore. Kyrie was now added to that list.

---

*Chapter Three*

---

"Everyone, split into groups of sixteen. You will do your bond-building activities in and with this group. One faculty member will sit with each group. I will distribute the list of activities. You don't have to do them in order, but everyone needs to participate in all activities." Mr. Black announced.

We all did as he said. Thankfully, I was in a group with my friends. I didn't know everyone else in the group, but I didn't need to know them. Mr. Brown was our group leader.

"All right everyone, we have our list. Do you want me to read off the activities, or do you want to do them in order?"

Everyone voted that we do them in order.

"Ok, we will go around the circle in a clockwise motion. The first activity is an ice breaker question. What race(s) experience the most discrimination?" Mr. Brown sat and stared at as waiting for a response, but everyone remained silent.

"Come on guys, we need to do these activities. We have a lot to accomplish before the school day ends, so participate please."

Brent Randall cleared his throat and said, "The only races discriminated against are the ones who let it happen to themselves. I'm not responsible for anyone else's actions, so I don't know why I'm being forced to talk about this."

Four others simultaneously said, "Agreed."

As Mr. Brown continued through the group, I quickly realized how prevalent racism, prejudice, and ignorance really were.

Finally, he made it to my friends. "Nyssa, what's your answer?"

"I think discrimination happens to everyone, but I believe it happens to certain races more than others. African Americans experience a lot of discrimination. So do Mexicans. I have seen it firsthand, and I don't agree with it. Still, I find it difficult to speak up because I don't want to be dragged into a bad situation." Nyssa shrugged her shoulders and hung her head.

Mr. Brown looked at me. "Mr. Brown, I don't want to answer this question or any question about race. Discrimination happens. People don't get to choose whether they are discriminated against or not. People learned how to overcome it, how to fight against it, and how to keep from being discriminatory against others. That's all I have to say."

"Emmitt, how about you?"

"My dad is a police officer. He works at the same precinct as the officer who killed Kyrie. My dad said what happened was a discriminatory act of prejudice that quickly turned into a racism fueled hate crime. I hate that discrimination is still a thing. So much time has passed since slavery and segregation, but not much has changed. Things need to improve, but that requires people to make an effort that many refuse to give."

As the day continued, the topics and conversations grew deeper and deeper. As I listened to everyone speak, I realized that there were many subtle undertones of prejudice and racism on all sides, but not everyone in the conversation was guilty of those things.

The final activity for the day was introspection. We were all handed a questionnaire with ten questions. We were not supposed to put our names on the papers because all answers were to remain anonymous. It took about an hour

for all of us to complete the questionnaire.
Once we were finished, Mr. Brown
collected each paper. When the final
paper was handed in, he mixed up the
order of the papers and handed one to
each of us.

"You will now read aloud the papers I
have handed you." Mr. Brown said firmly.

As everyone read, the answers revealed
the true state of our hearts. Some of the
answers angered us. Others left us
questioning the way we viewed the world.
Many answers left us sad, but only one set
of answers left everyone speechless.

"Brent, please read your paper."

Brent stood up and read,

"What does the world think about you?

'The world thinks I am worthless because of my color.'

What is something you would change about yourself if you could?

'I would change my race. I would change my color.'"

Brent looked bewildered at what he was reading, but he continued.

"If you could change one thing to make the world a better place, what would you change?

'I would make everyone the same color.'"

"Brent, this is not a time to joke. Hand me the paper and sit down. Since you are not taking this activity seriously, I will read the paper."

Mr. Brown looked at the first three answers and realized Brent wasn't making light of the situation at all.

"Brent, I apologize for my response. I am not going to put anyone else on the spot, but whoever is responsible for the answers on these sheets, I would advise that you speak to the head of the support group before you leave here today."

Mr. Brown did not finish reading the paper because he could see how upset everyone was. Well, everyone except me because I wrote that paper.

All that the assembly did was show me that I was right for making the decision I had made. I was counting down the minutes until school was finished. I could not wait to get home.

"Wow, that assembly was powerful, wasn't it?" Nyssa asked as we got into Emmitt's car.

"I guess. I'm just glad it's over."

Nyssa and Emmitt looked at each other but did not say anything in response.

"What? Why are you guys looking at each other?"

They still said nothing.

"Seriously, what?"

"Promise you won't get offended and we'll answer you."

"I promise, Nyssa."

"Ok, we are just concerned about you."

"Why?"

"Because we know that paper was yours. You are beautiful. You don't need to change anything about yourself. The world is evil, but you're not. Your friends and family know that you're a good person. We love you for you and for who you are. That means we also love that you're Black because that's a part of you. We've been respectful of the fact that you're still coping with the loss of your father. That's why we never said anything to you, but you need to know that you are beautiful." Nyssa looked at me in the rearview mirror and quickly stopped talking.

"Nyssa is right, Renee. We love you no matter what you decide, and we'll support you no matter what. Ok?"

"Ok."

Emmitt began to pull out of the parking spot when he heard someone screaming,

"Stop! Wait! Stop!"

We turned around and saw Mrs. James running towards us.

"Renee, Renee Wilson?"

"Yes ma'am?"

"Hi sweetheart, I wanted to speak with you earlier, but I didn't get a chance to. I wanted to give you a hug. I also wanted to let you know that I knew your father. He was a good man. How are you and your mother doing?" Mrs. James said.

"We are doing ok," I said.

I got out of Emmitt's car to give her a hug, but I dropped my bag. Everything fell out on the ground. As she bent down to help me pick everything up, she saw my makeup and my new bath bleach. She looked very upset when she handed my things back to me.

"I'm going to let you go, but I have one more thing to tell you."

"Yes ma'am?"

"Love the skin that you're in. That is what your father would have wanted." Mrs. James looked me in the eyes and took me by the hand.

"Thank you, I will. Before you go, may I ask you a question?"

"Sure, you can ask me anything."

"What was the name of the officer who killed your son?"

"Callahan, Benjamin Callahan."

---

*Chapter Four*

---

I was floored when Mrs. James told me the name of her son's killer. I was curious to know if he was related to the officer who killed my dad.

The entire way home I researched everything I could find on Kyrie James. Watchlook was filled with Kyrie James hashtags, and even after 12 years, people were still hashtagging my father's name. During my search, I discovered a group named Black Wives Matter. It was a support group for widows of Black men who were killed due to racism. I found several other groups for Black movements throughout my state and across the nation. As I read through the posts and looked at the pictures, I finally felt like I wasn't alone.

So many Black teenagers were posting about not wanting to be Black anymore. A few had actually used the bath bleach, but they still weren't happy. One girl had used bath bleach for three years. She looked so fair-skinned in her photos. I had a hard time believing that the bleach had worked so well. I sent her a private message to ask her about her experience with the bath bleach and how society has reacted toward her.

*Hi, I'm Renee, I was wondering if you are ok with answering a few questions. I'm contemplating using bath bleach, and I am curious about the reactions of the people in your circle. I look forward to hearing from you. Thank you.*

I didn't expect to hear from her for a while if at all, so I went back to scrolling through posts. I looked at the girl's pictures again and began to read the comments.

*Why would you change your complexion? Black is beautiful.*

**This saddens me. We should not have to change ourselves for acceptance. No one else does that.**

*You still look beautiful, but remember changing your complexion doesn't change your features. It is still apparent that you are Black.*

***Anyone considering this needs to reconsider doing it immediately. You will not receive acceptance from those you are trying to fit in with, and you are alienating yourself from your Black community by trying to hide the fact that you are Black.***

After reading the comments on her posts, I was glad she hadn't responded. The comments answered most of my questions. It was clear that lightening up was frowned upon. I was about to sign out of Watchlook when a message notification popped up on my screen.

*Hey Renee, I saw your message. I'm Erica. It's nice to meet you. I have answers for you. Hopefully, they will help with your decision making. I do not regret my choice, but I do regret my choice. I wanted to be less of a target, but now a larger target is on my back than before. Black people can see that my complexion is not natural which tells them that I am unhappy in my own skin. Other races notice than I am Black, and they give me a hard time about it. Believe it or not, I get picked on more than I used to. If I could go back, I would do things differently. I probably would have changed my complexion but not to this extent. I hope this helps. Be sure to keep in touch and let me know how things work out for you.*

Little did I know that this would be the start of a lifelong friendship.

Between Erica's message and the comments, I was able to make up my mind. I took the bath bleach into the bathroom and poured it down the drain. Afterward, I went through my purse, bedroom, and bathroom. I found all of the makeup I had been buying to lighten up, and I threw it in the trash.

When my mom got home, she found me on the bathroom floor crying.

"Renee, what's wrong?"

"I'm sorry, Mom. I'm so sorry." I cried as I fell into her arms.

"Did something happen at school? Do I need to call your principal?"

"Yes and no."

"Ok, I'll leave it alone for now. Let me help you up off the floor. Come sit in the kitchen with me while I make you some cocoa."

I did as my mom said, but I couldn't stop crying. Every time I tried to open my mouth, words wouldn't come out of it. I wasn't sure how to tell my mom all of the things I had come to realize.

"Mom, I'm sorry. I'm so sorry. I have been giving you such a hard time. I haven't been considering how I have been making you feel. I lost my dad, but you lost the love of your life. You've been putting up with my nonsense for so long, and I want you to know I'm sorry, and I'm going to learn how to love myself again."

"Thank you, Renee," she said as she handed me my cocoa.

"I know it was hard for you. You and your dad were the best of friends. I know he loved you with his whole heart. I know you loved him just as much. I hurt for myself, but I hurt for you so much more. I still do. I had my time with the man of my dreams. We were together from the time we were 15. Martin died young, but I had a life with him for 11 years. You only had him for four years baby. Believe me, I understand."

My mom and I stayed up talking all night. We went through the garage and brought in boxes of photo albums and picture frames that used to be in our home. The once painful reminder of our loss was now putting smiles on our faces as we reminisced.

The next morning when I woke up, I knew what I needed to do. I asked my mom for Mrs. James' phone number.

"Hi, Mrs. James, It's Renee, Renee Wilson. I was wondering if I can meet you today. There is something I need to speak with you about."

"Hello, Renee, you sound much better than you did yesterday. Of course, we can meet. Let's grab lunch, my treat."

After picking a place, we hung up, and I went to get dressed.

I met Mrs. James in the Downtown District. I hadn't been in that area for a while. When I pulled up to the building, I was surprised to find that there was a mural of my daddy and me painted on the restaurant wall. It was the same picture he had as his Watchlook profile picture.

"Hi, Renee, I had you meet me here so you could see this. The restaurant owner has dedicated this property to the remembrance of the slain victims of police brutality. My Kyrie will have his mural on the wall next week."

"Wow, Mrs. James, thank you for showing me this. How are you coping with everything?"

"I miss my baby so much. It's so hard not having him here. I miss his laugh and his jokes. I miss the way his eyes lit up when he smiled. This is a tough situation, but I'm hoping and praying that justice prevails. In the meantime, I'm taking things one day at a time."

"That is understandable. I actually asked you to meet me in hopes of finding justice for your son. I did a lot of searching online last night. The man who shot your son is the younger brother of the man who shot my father. I also have some information for you to give to your lawyer. Based on what I read online, this information will significantly help your case."

As tears streamed down her face, Mrs. James replied, "Thank you, Renee. You will never know how much this means to me."

We hugged and parted ways.

---

*Chapter Five*

---

Over the course of the next few weeks, I talked to Mrs. James daily. We had grown very close in such a short time, and she had really helped me through a lot of problems I had been dealing with for quite a while.

After losing my father, I had a hard time believing that Jesus really loved me as much as He said He did. I watched my mother go through a lot of pain and hurt at the hands of people claiming to be His people, people who claimed to be her friends. My mother, Ruby Jean, was a minister in our local church when my father was murdered. She had been attending every event on the church calendar and was in charge of the Regional Outreach Ministry for our organization. She was very well known and always had people around her, at least until my father died. At the time, I was too little to realize that my mother was battling with depression. Her desire to be active in the church was diminished. Many of the people who called to check on her were the same ones who never spoke out about her husband's death. She spent a lot of time on Watchlook scrolling through posts trying to take her mind off of her pain, but in the process, she ended up more hurt than distracted.

My mother went to leave comments on her friends' pages and found that her once

"friends" were posting Watchlook
thoughts that said,

*Saying Black Lives Matter is racist.*

*If he had been more respectful, he'd still be
alive.*

*The police only kill you if you give them a
reason to.*

*Stop posting videos of this man dying. We
don't want to see that. Here's a recipe from
Pin Pages that will make your day!*

*Black people die every day and are killed
by other Black people. What's the
difference? You people need to lighten up.*

I remember walking into her room one
night after sitting outside of her door
listening to her sob for an hour. I was only
seven, but I knew what heartbreak

sounded like. I opened her door quietly and tiptoed into her room. I saw her computer screen, and I saw the posts. Moreover, I recognized the faces responsible for those posts, and it was that moment when I decided I wanted nothing to do with church, church people, or Jesus. I held my mother as she cried herself to sleep that night and many nights after that.

As I laid there with her, I wondered if the people posting had forgotten what happened to my father. I wondered if they were racist. I wondered if they were just smiling faces hating other races. It never made sense to me that they were always joking with my mother and father at events and services all the while feeling nothing but apathy and prejudice towards them.

Mrs. James understood exactly where I was coming from, but she reminded me that Jesus died for us because of the choices we make.

She said, "These people might not see how divisive they are. Although they have a right to feel however they want to feel, they might not realize that some of those feelings are wrong and are tearing the body of Christ apart. Many prejudices are learned and engrained. As children, we just see other children. We are not concerned about what they look like. We are concerned about the important things. Are they nice? Do they want to be my friends? Am I happy around them? We are not verbalizing these things, but those are the things we look for as children. However, that changes as we get older because of what we see, hear, and learn. Do not let these things shift your focus from what's important. Jesus is what's important. Let hypocrites be hypocrites. Let racists be racists. Let yourself be in the hands of the God who loves you and made you. I wrote a poem about you the day after we spoke in the parking lot, and I want to share it with you.

Black girl, Black girl,

Where'd you go?

Why didn't you want

The world to know?

Why wouldn't you let

Your color show?

Black girl, Black girl,

Don't you know

The way you shine

The way you glow?

The hurt you have,

Let it go

And trust in the One

Who holds your soul."

I immediately felt a weight lift off of me as I listened to the words she said. Mrs. James was a blessing to me, and I never would have had a relationship with her if not for the tragedy that had befallen us both.

After the conversation, I decided to pray for the first time in a long time. It was awkward, and I didn't feel like I was saying the right things. Nonetheless, I still said what I could, and as each day passed, I began to say more. I prayed daily that God would bring justice for the James family, and one Tuesday morning, I received a phone call from Mrs. James.

"Officer Benjamin Callahan is finally in police custody and is awaiting trial." She said as soon as I answered the phone.

Mrs. James was praying for justice to be served because she didn't want to see what would happen in the community if it wasn't.

"Renee, dear, what is happening in our nation right now is terrible. It feels like the world has shifted. Things are so upside down. With every day it looks like we are actively regressing. My parents used to tell me stories of what life was like during the pre-Civil Rights Movement. Much of what is happening today is just like in those times."

"I couldn't agree more, Mrs. James. Last night, I posted a status on Watchlook about your son's life mattering, and within five minutes, my post was filled with hateful comments telling me that I am anti-police and racist. I don't understand why people treat us this way."

"Dear, we won't ever understand, but we have to trust that God sees and knows. He is not sleeping. We can't give up. We've fought too hard for too long. Just have faith, God will bring us through."

I hung up the phone and went to find my mom. She was sitting in the living room crying and yelling, "Why God! Why?"

"Mom, what happened?"

"Another unarmed Black man was killed by a police officer. That man was a friend of your father's."

I took my phone out of my pocket and pulled up my Watchlook page.

"Let me guess, his name was Joe Simon?"

"Yes, it was. How did you...?"

"Because he's another hashtag. Mom, I'm tired of us being turned into hashtags."

"I am too."

As we sat inside watching the news, a loud uproar began to pour through our windows. My mom went to pull the blinds and looked out of the window.

"Renee, come quick!"

I hurried over to her and saw hundreds of people pouring on to the street with signs and megaphones.

"Justice for Kyrie James!"

"Justice for Joe Simon!"

"Stop killing us!"

"Speak up! Speak out!"

The street was overflowing with people of all different races and colors. It was actually quite beautiful to see people coming together for a cause.

We decided to drive over to City Hall to watch the protest unfold. When we arrived, we were surprised to find thousands of people gathered. Countless times, Black men, women, and children were wrongfully killed, but outrage was only seen in and from the Black community. This time things were different. Something about the deaths of Kyrie and Joe sparked a fire in the once quiet people of our town. Maybe it was due to the fact that both Joe and Kyrie were prominent figures in their communities. Maybe it was due to them having such an impact on so many lives, or maybe it was because they were Christians who fought the good fight and ended up brutally murdered.

Thoughts continued to circulate in my mind as I sat waiting to see what would happen next.

---

*Chapter Six*

---

"Attention, may I have everyone's attention please." A voice called out over the loudspeakers.

"Thank you all for gathering today. I am happy to see so many faces I recognize and so many that I don't. We have all come here for one thing, justice! We are hoping that the officers who have killed Kyrie James and Joe Simon will receive punishment for their actions. This world is in chaos, and we want the cycle to end. How many Black men, women, and children must be killed before people speak out? I have seen outrage about many things. I have seen changes made because enough people spoke out about the things that were bothering them. This prejudice, injustice, and racism should have been spoken out against ages ago, but it needs to be understood that our community can't be the only ones speaking. I can tell my children to behave. They are my children. I can tell my nieces and nephews to behave. They are my family. I can tell my students to behave. They are in my care, but I cannot tell someone else's children to behave if I do not have that person's support or permission. This issue works the same way. I have no authority in your home, at your job, or during your family gatherings. I have no voice in those environments because they are not my own, but you do. You have the means and power to change things in your environment. Never forget that you should be the change you want to see."

Each speech was as powerful as the last. The crowd continued to grow until City Hall was surrounded by protesters seeking justice.

The last speaker of the day headed to the front of the crowd. It was Mrs. James. Although she was clearly emotional, she was able to deliver the most beautiful speech I had ever heard.

"Thank you for your support. It is beautiful to see everyone here for the same cause with the same goal, justice. However, the goal I hope we can all look toward is unity. We must be united in this cause and the challenges that lie ahead.

Grieving my son has been difficult. I see his face nightly in my dreams, but I see him daily on the television screen, on my email homepage, and on my smartphone. I have had very few moments to myself. Finding peace, at this time, is challenging especially when reporters are at my door because I didn't answer their phone calls. Nonetheless, I will press on. We need to press on. My son is gone, but I don't want anyone else to have to grieve a child, spouse, parent, or loved one. The only way to stop this is to call out injustice, oppression, and racism as soon as you see it. Don't wait for someone else to do it. Once the moment has passed it is too late. Our community is hurting. We are grieving the loss of hundreds of lives we have seen taken on video. Imagine how many others have died, and no one knows what happened because there was no one there to record. We cannot continue this way. Being just another trending hashtag should never be the outcome of a short-lived life. It is time for us to stand together. We need to commit to standing and staying together until the heart, mind, and sin problem is no longer the norm."

Camera crews had arrived to broadcast the protest as the local news stations sent reporters to interview the speakers and family of Kyrie James.

For the next two days, protests were popping up all across the nation. Watchlook was finally filled with more love and support for the Black community than hate.

*These tragedies have got to stop. No one should have to live in fear.*

*The world has come so far in technological and medical advances, it's sad that we could figure out those things but still can't figure out how to treat others.*

*This is how I see this situation. A Black person looks at the table and sees 15 empty seats. The Black person goes to sit down at the table, but is immediately told, 'Don't take my seat! I worked hard for my seat.'*

*'I wasn't trying to take your seat. I was going to sit in one of the empty ones.'*

*'I said don't take my seat!'*

The world finally felt like people were coming together and were willing to see things as they are and have been for the

Black community for the last 500 plus years. It was nothing short of amazing until one unidentified man threw a brick through a storefront window.

No one knew who the man was or what he looked like, but that didn't matter. With one brick, everything changed. Protesters were being blamed for the outburst of riots across the nation. The once inspiring posts of support, acknowledgment, and love quickly changed to blame, hatred, and jesting at the state of the Black community. The fickleness of the world was starting to show, but thankfully, those who vowed to stand with us continued to stand because they understood what the true issue was.

*You ruined your chances to have your voices heard.*

*You criminals are the reason your lives are as bad as they are.*

*Dr. King never acted like this. He never did these things. You are looters. You should be ashamed of yourselves. Look at what you're doing.*

Although the protests in my town and many other towns stayed peaceful, that was no longer the focus. The news crews drove away without even doing what they came to do. Mr. and Mrs. James never had the opportunity to share their thoughts with the world because the world was beginning to turn on them once again.

---

*Chapter Seven*

---

The streets were now quiet because all of the protests in my town were dismantled.

Someone showed up and threw a rock at one of the police cars while we were still protesting. The police told everyone to leave immediately. Because we didn't want any trouble and we had seen everything happening in the news, we left the scene. Thankfully, the police caught the person responsible for throwing the rock, but the identity of the person had remained unknown to the public.

It was strange resuming life as normal. I had been spending a lot of time in my house post the protests. People were angry and hurting. Fires were being set throughout the city, but no one knew who was setting them. A curfew had been enacted due to riots, violence, and looting. My mom and I agreed that we should not go out unless it was an emergency. Most of the town was functioning the same way. People were only leaving homes for work, emergencies, and essentials, and everyone was back inside by 7:00 pm. The world had become such a scary place, and I knew it was going to get worse if justice didn't prevail.

As I sat pondering a simpler life and time, my laptop started ringing. Emmitt and Nyssa were calling me on SeeMyFace.

"Hey, guys, what's up?"

"I don't know. Emmitt called me and said he had something urgent to tell us."

"Oh ok, Emmitt, what did you want to tell us?"

"Before I say anything, you both need to put in headphones, and you cannot repeat anything I tell you to anyone. Do you understand?"

"Yes."

"I have been at the police station with my dad for the last few days. He doesn't want me at home by myself with all the craziness that is going on. While I was there, I overheard a conversation."

"Ok...what was it?" Nyssa asked impatiently.

"Remember the guy who threw the rock at the police car?"

"Yeah…" I said with anticipation.

"It was Callahan. The other Callahan." Emmitt said stone-faced.

"The one who killed my father?"

"Yes, but no one knows why he did it." He replied.

"Wow, that is so crazy," Nyssa said.

"I know right."

"I'm really sorry, Renee. Are you ok?" Nyssa asked.

"Honestly, I don't know. I knew he was free, but I always imagined that he moved elsewhere. Knowing that he is so close has me a little unsettled."

"Don't worry, Renee, I won't let anything happen to you." Emmitt winked.

Nyssa rolled her eyes and laughed.

"So, on a lighter note, I finally got my license!"

"Congratulations Nyssa!" I replied.

"Yeah, congrats! If we weren't locked down, I'd let you drive my car."

"Really?" Nyssa asked in shock.

"Of course! You'd sit in the front seat with the car in park. You could move the steering wheel a little, but that's it." Emmitt laughed so hard.

I couldn't help but laugh, even Nyssa chuckled.

It was nice to have something to take my mind off of everything going on in the world. I was grateful for my friends because I never had to question where they stood. They were always standing with me.

I stayed on the phone with them until my mom called me for dinner. Usually, we ate at the dinner table, but my mom wanted to eat and watch the news together. While we were eating, Breaking News, came across the screen.

"Protests and riots are happening all across the nation as the Black community cries out for justice. Details surface in the Sasha Blue case. New footage has been released."

It was crazy to see protests in so many countries. The movement was spreading, and people were beginning to wake up.

As more and more videos surfaced on Watchlook, people were voicing outrage.

Friends and families were calling out prejudice among themselves, and the truth was being revealed as the silent continued to remain silent.

When the news went to a commercial break, I looked at my mom and said, "Mom, can we go to church on Sunday?"

"Church? Sure. May I ask why you've had this sudden change of heart?"

"After talking to Mrs. James, I realized that my anger towards Jesus was misplaced, and I made my heart right with Him."

"Of course, we can go to church. You should probably find your outfit before bed since tomorrow is Sunday."

"Oh, I didn't realize. I'll go get my outfit right now."

I could hardly sleep. I was so excited to return to church for the first time in years.

---

## Chapter Eight

---

"Get up, Renee! Renee! We're gonna be late. I've been trying to get you up for an hour now."

"Mom, I'm tired. Stop please."

"Ok, I guess we're not going to church today."

As soon as her words processed, I jumped out of bed and got ready for church. Fifteen minutes later, we were on the way.

When we pulled into the parking lot, I saw so many faces that looked familiar, but I didn't remember who they were.

We walked into the church and were greeted by the Head Usher, Sis. Suzette.

"Good morning, welcome to the Church of Christ in Love." She said as she shook my hand.

As soon as she looked at my mom, her mouth dropped. "Sis. Ruby Jean, it has been quite some time since we've seen you."

"Yes, it has Sis. Suzette." My mom smiled and walked past her.

We went to find a seat and soon realized we had shown up to a special event Sunday. All of the sister churches in the area were represented at the service. All of my mother's former friends were in the church. I felt horrible for asking her to come, but she seemed unbothered.

"Mom, are you ok?"

"Yes. Why wouldn't I be?"

"Don't you see who is here?"

"I do, and they also see me." She looked at me, smiled, and sat back in her seat.

The service was really long but good. Every church had a part in the service. Pastor Webber's sermon was very well-timed. God knew what needed to be said. "Church, we are at a crossroads. We can head to paved roads or to the cliff's edge, but that is a choice we all have to make for ourselves. We can choose love, or we can let the hatred continue to spread throughout ourselves and our flock. I do my best not to be active on social media, but my wife and children are. They have shown me the things said by congregation members and church leaders. Brothers and sisters, these things should not be. Racism is pervasive, and it is rampant in our churches. Racism did not die with the Civil Rights Movement. I have experienced racism both as a little boy and as a man. I have seen it affect my friends and my family. I have seen it drive a wedge between our members. It has caused us to lose members both to death and to hurt. This should not be. We can all quote 1 John 4:7-8, but do we live it? His Word is plain. There is no room for interpretation in these verses. We have got to get it together before God has to step in and deal with us..."

By the time Pastor Webber had finished his sermon, the only dry eyes in the room belonged to the people continuously doing the things he had mentioned.

After service was a luncheon, and everyone was invited. I told my mom that I was content going home, but she said we were going to stay.

Before we went to the hall, Pastor Webber pulled my mom aside and said, "I knew that the Word would not go down smoothly today, but when I saw you walk in, I knew God had given me this sermon for a much larger purpose."

My mom smiled and nodded, but she didn't say anything else. We walked next door and quickly found a seat. People were staring at us, and I felt extremely awkward. Nonetheless, my mother wasn't. She knew what to expect after she saw the other churches who were present. Her once friends were now gawkers whispering but saying nothing to her, and she didn't care. She spoke with and to the friends who had kept in touch with her throughout the years, and she was happy doing so. I had never been so proud.

Finally, one woman did approach her. Sis. Teresa walked over and said, "Hi Ruby, it's good to see you. You look well. What happened that made you disappear for so long?"

My mother looked her in the face and said, "My husband died, and after his death, the support just wasn't there. However, the Watchlook posts were, and I saw each and every one of them. That is what made me leave."

Sis. Teresa was mortified. She walked away and never looked at my mom again.

I was surprised that my mom was able to keep her cool, but it seemed like she was prepared for everything that was thrown at her.

When it was time to leave, my mom said her goodbyes and left amicably.

After watching my mother interact with the women who claimed to be her friends so long ago, I realized that the hurt she felt didn't get the best of her. She had found a way to move on, and I knew then that moving on could bring healing even in the worst of situations.

My mom could see that the gears in my head were turning.

"Renee, I saw your face today during service. You need to get your face under control. I was not bothered by the presence of a single person in that church. After losing your father, I learned very quickly who was for me. Young people can be very naïve when it comes to the ways of the world, so let this be a lesson for you. Anyone can fake a smile, a laugh, or a friendship, but when people show you who they are, don't wait around hoping that they'll show you something different. I love every person who was in that church today, but loving people doesn't mean that I need to surround myself with toxic petty nonsense. I forgive all of the people who hurt me, but I will not pretend that my friendships with them are restored. That is why I responded the way that I did. False pretenses are no different than lying, and deception in the church can be very divisive. I serve God. I follow God. I'm not following any man, and I'm not going to let any man drag me to the pits of Hell over unforgiveness and facades. Do you understand what I am saying?"

"Yes ma'am."

"Ok, thank you. You also need to learn how to fix your face when encountered with situations like that."

---

*Chapter Nine*

---

Several days had passed since the curfew had lifted. Protests had formed again, but this time the police were present and supporting the cause. Several of our elected officials came and held press conferences to spread the purpose of our protests and to announce plans that would soon be enacted to prevent future deaths caused by racism.

All over the world, people were speaking out and protesting for justice as well. Prominent figures and celebrities were using their platforms as a place to reach their fans and others about the racism binding their countries.

Although there was still evil in the world, the good was beginning to outshine it.

My mom had invited Mrs. James to our home. I was able to invite my friends as well. We had a cookout and sat in the living room awaiting the verdict in the case of Officer Benjamin Callahan.

The news was spending much time focusing on other things. We weren't sure if they were stalling or if they hadn't heard any updates. Several hours had passed before we finally heard the Breaking News alert.

The news anchor said, "A verdict has been made in the case of Kyrie James. After long deliberation, a jury of his peers found Officer Benjamin Callahan guilty of manslaughter. Sentencing has not been awarded at this time. He will be taken to prison immediately and will serve his allotted sentence with no opportunity for early release."

We weren't sure whether to celebrate or not because we didn't know what prison sentencing usually accompanied manslaughter. However, Emmitt was able to explain.

Mrs. James was not saddened by the sentence; she even led a prayer for Benjamin Callahan asking God to help him find Jesus in prison.

I was saddened that he wasn't going to receive a longer sentence, but I thought back to the sentencing of his brother in my father's case.

Mrs. James could see the sadness in my eyes. She took me by the hand and said, "Renee, I am ok. I will continue to be ok. Don't be sad for Kyrie. He is spending eternity with our Heavenly Father. No one can hurt him anymore."

I smiled at Mrs. James and nodded because I couldn't say a single word without crying. I never found out if Mrs. James believed that she had received justice or not. Nevertheless, I knew she was ok with what had happened.

The Joe Simon case was yet to be resolved. We continued to protest because our plight needed to be heard. I had been focused on Kyrie James and my father. I hadn't even watched the video of Joe Simon's death until Kyrie's case was closed. As I sat and watched Joe Simon pleading for his life, my heart broke once again. Joe was a 38-year-old father of four. He was the Youth Pastor at his local church. Joe was on his way to visit one of his kids from youth group when a truck pulled up behind him and ran him off of the road. Joe was slightly injured in the crash, but he was able to escape his vehicle before it rolled.

When he got out of the vehicle, two men were standing over him and another man was recording. They didn't realize that other people had seen what happened and were also recording from a distance.

The two men beat Joe senselessly as Joe begged them to let him go home to his wife and kids. Nonetheless, they didn't. By the time the police arrived, Joe had already stopped breathing. His final words were Jesus keep my family safe.

I could not believe the things that were being done to my community just because of what we looked like. It was baffling to me that the way I was born angered people and made them feel as though I didn't deserve to have a voice, to have rights, or to live.

After watching the video of Joe Simon's death, I prayed nightly that justice would be served. His death sparked outrage in people who were once silent, and riots or not, it was clear what side of the fence people were on.

Several people at my local church knew Joe very well. We had a vigil for him in the

park, but it was interrupted when a lady
called the police on us for assembling
suspiciously.

When the officers arrived and observed
what we were doing, they detained the
woman until the local news was able to
send a reporter and crew to the park.

The reporter interviewed her and asked
her why she called the police. She replied,
"I...I don't...I don't know. I just felt like I
should. I've never seen people gathering
in the park with candles and I was afraid
they might start fires like those rioters on
TV."

The camera crew showed the police
putting the woman into the back of their
vehicle. Before the officers drove away,

Officer Delaney Grey, Emmitt's father, spoke with the reporter on the air.

"The sheriff was unable to come because he is handling more pressing matters at this time. He sent me down here to deliver this message. 'I want to make it known that anyone in this town who calls the police on a Black person for no reason will be fined and arrested for wasting department resources and for keeping officers from doing their jobs. We are not here for you to call us every time you see a Black person eating at a restaurant, using the gym, swimming in a public pool, or walking a dog. None of these things are a threat to you. None of these things are endangering anyone, but you are when you make calls like this. My officers will not be used as prejudice patrol. If you are prejudice, leave us out of it and just go home before you make a fool of yourself on national television."

We were thankful that our local sheriff decided to crack down on unnecessary 911 calls. Knowing that we didn't have to live in fear of people getting away with reporting us for nothing was a much-needed step in the right direction.

After the vigil, my mom and I were headed home when sirens went off behind us. We both were praying that Jesus would intervene before potential escalation.

When the officer approached the window, I was filming, and my mother had both hands in the air. She had put her license and registration on the dashboard before he even had to ask.

As soon as he saw my mother's hands in the air, he became teary-eyed and said, "Ma'am, you don't have to do that. I'm not a bad cop. I don't need to see your license or registration. I saw that you had a taillight out, and I have a spare one in my car. I pulled you over to let you know that and to ask if it's ok for me to replace it for you."

My mom slowly put her hands down and said, "Of course officer, thank you."

I continued to record live on Watchlook. I knew all police officers were not bad, but I wanted the world to see what this officer was doing. Officer Goodman replaced the light for us. He stood and chatted with us for a while. When he saw my mom, he recognized her from the video of the day my dad died.

Officer Goodman's actions went viral, and I was glad that they did.

The world had been flooded with negative imagery of Black people and of police officers, and I had vowed to be a part of the solution.

---

*Chapter Ten*

---

*Ring Ring*

*Ring Ring*

I rushed down the hall to grab my phone. By the time I had gotten to it, I had five missed calls from Emmitt. I started to dial his number when my phone rang again.

"Hello"

"Renee, I'm so glad I finally reached you. I'm five minutes from your house. Are you dressed to go out?"

"No, I'm not, but I can be."

"Ok, I'll see you soon."

I got dressed as quickly as I could and rushed out the door.

"Hey Emmitt, where's Nyssa?"

"She has a doctor's appointment."

"Oh ok, where are we going?"

"It's a surprise, but we have to get there in ten minutes."

Emmitt had never looked so excited. He was driving erratically to make sure we would arrive on time.

"Slow down, Emmitt, slow down."

He didn't listen, but we still made it safely.

"Come on, hurry," he said as he jumped out of the car and took off running into the park.

I did not know where we were going, so I did not dress sensibly for the occasion.

"Hold on, I can't run through grass in heels!" I yelled as I pulled my shoes off and started running.

When I caught up to Emmitt, there was a large crowd gathered including my mom and Mrs. James.

Mayor Blanchett was standing on a podium next to something covered by a tarp.

She looked out into the crowd, cleared her throat, and said, "May I please have everyone's attention?"

The crowd silenced instantaneously.

"Thank you everyone for gathering today. So much has been going on in our town, nation, and world lately that really makes me question the state of humanity, but I am proud to see that our town has been steadily coming together. We are gathered here today to unveil a reminder of the changes we are making and the reason why."

The mayor stepped off of the podium and pulled the tarp down unveiling a statue of Kyrie James and my father with a placard that said Wilson James Park.

Mayor Blanchett returned to the podium and said, "Wilson James Park will now and forever serve as a tribute to those wrongfully slain."

The crowd cheered and applauded. Mayor Blanchett walked off of the podium and

came to shake hands with Mr. and Mrs.
James, my mother, and me.

We stayed in the park for a while for the

celebration ceremony that followed the
unveiling of the statue.

My mom and I left earlier than everyone
else because we had planned a trip out of
town. My mom had reached out to Mrs.
Simon about coming for a visit. As soon as
my mom heard from her, we made
preparations to leave.

The trip was long, but we made it safely.
By the time we arrived, it was very late, so
we all went to bed. The next morning, we
all got acquainted. It was nice to hear
stories about my father from Mrs. Simon.
Her children had a lot of questions about
how I coped with my father's death. I was

thankful that I was able to offer support and answers.

In the few days we were together, we became very close. My mom and I also learned a lot of information about Joe's case that hadn't become public as of yet.

The men responsible for killing Joe were former police officers, but they were also supremacists.

The attorney representing Joe wanted the case to be tried as a hate crime. However, that type of charge was very rare in these types of cases. His family was just hoping for justice whether or not the case was tried as a hate crime.

The days had flown by quickly. It was time for us to leave. We said our goodbyes and were on our way again. On the way back to town, we heard another news story of a Black woman being wrongfully killed by the police while relaxing in her home. Her name was Tasha Angel. She was a doctor at Memorial General Hospital. She was a pediatric surgeon. She was also a wife and a mother of two. The video of her death surfaced while we were visiting the Simons. My mom and I had yet to see it, but we planned to watch it as soon as we got home.

Once we got home and went inside, we watched the bodycam footage of Tasha Angel's death. Social media was flooded with angry people of all races and colors crying out once again for justice.

The cries were loud and powerful. People's voices were finally being heard, and action was promptly taken. It did not take weeks or months for a verdict to be made in Tasha's case. The officers responsible for her death were investigated, fired, and incarcerated in a week's time. The officer who shot her was charged with first-degree murder. The other officers were charged with lesser but fair sentences.

We finally felt as though justice had been served. The Simon case was still underway, and we continued to pray for a positive and just outcome.

The community once again held a vigil, and this time, no one called the police on us.

Protesting continued over the next few weeks, and social media and the news

continued to cover the revolution that
was taking place. More and more people
continued to stand up, speak out, and join
the cause. The Wednesday morning
before the case was closed, I woke up to
find that a Check Your Privilege Challenge
was trending and circulating all across
social media platforms. People shared
some very revealing information as they
searched within themselves and
compared their lives to Black lives. The
level of vulnerability seen in the videos
posted was beautiful. Instead of the voices
quieting over time, they were growing
louder and stronger than ever.

It was now Thursday, the day that the
verdict would be announced. As we
awaited the verdict of Joe Simon's case,
the world stood silent. Joe's death had

touched his city, his country, and the world. He was now a symbol of what life looked like for Blacks when no one spoke out against injustice. His death touched lives all over the world, and it led to progress and change.

Breaking News flashed across the TV screen one more time. My heart felt like it was pounding out of my chest. I held my mother's hand as we braced ourselves for the outcome.

"The jury has found the men involved in the death of Joe Simon guilty of first-degree murder and a hate crime. The assailants will spend life in prison."

Justice was finally served, and many changes were to come to ensure that justice would continue to prevail.

## About the Author

The author has chosen not to include her biography in this book because the book and the message of the book are not meant to promote her in any way. She hopes this book will shed some light on what has been going on in the world. Her prayer is that everyone can find common ground and learn to live as one.